3 1170 00497 1929

BLACK NELL

BLACK NELL

The Adventures of a
COYOTE

SHIRLEY WOODS

ILLUSTRATED BY
CELIA GODKIN

A GROUNDWOOD BOOK
DOUGLAS & McINTYRE
VANCOUVER TORONTO BUFFALO

Glenview Public Library
1930 Glenview Road
Glenview, Illinois

Text copyright © 1998 by Shirley Woods
Illustrations copyright © 1998 by Celia Godkin

All rights reserved. No part of this book may be reproduced or
transmitted in any form or by any means, without the prior
written permission of the publisher or, in the case of photocopy-
ing or other reprographic copying, a licence from CANCOPY
(Canadian Reprography Collective), Toronto, Ontario.

Groundwood Books / Douglas & McIntyre Ltd.
585 Bloor Street West, Toronto, Ontario M6G 1K5

Distributed in the U.S.A. by Publishers Group West
4065 Hollis Street, Emeryville, CA 94608

We acknowledge the assistance of the Canada Council for the
Arts and the Ontario Arts Council for our publishing program.

Library of Congress Data is available

Canadian Cataloguing in Publication Data
Woods, Shirley E.
Black Nell: the adventures of a coyote
"A Groundwood book".
ISBN 0-88899-318-8 (bound) ISBN 0-88899-319-6 (pbk.)
I. Godkin, Celia. II. Title.
PS8595.0652B52 1998   jC813'.54   C97-932295-2
PZ7.W66Bl 1998

Illustrations by Celia Godkin
Design by Michael Solomon
Printed and bound in Canada by Webcom

MAR   5 1999

For my sister Jill

Contents

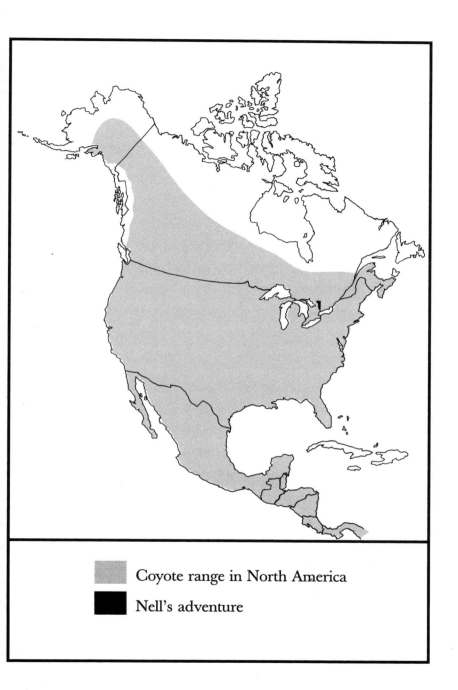

Coyote range in North America

Nell's adventure

CHAPTER 1

The Birth of a Coyote

B Y the third week of April, the snow had almost gone. Green shoots pushed through the faded grass, and there was a scent of spring in the air. In this land of forest and farms, it often rained during April. The rain soaked the plowed fields, shone the stones in the furrows and painted the bare trees black.

Nell was born on just such a rainy morning. But, at the moment of her birth, the sun broke through. It lit the entrance to her den and turned the water dripping from the branches into falling jewels. For an Eastern coyote, the sudden appearance of the sun was a lucky sign.

Nell was one of five in the litter. Each of the babies was the size of a small squirrel. They all had pug noses, floppy ears and short coats of gray fur. Except for Nell, whose coat was almost black.

The pups were born blind and wouldn't be able to see until they were ten days old. All they could manage was to snuggle up to their mother, who fed them with her milk and kept them warm with her body.

Nell's mother resembled a small wolf or a German shepherd dog. She had a pointed nose, upright ears, long legs and a bushy tail. Her coat was the color of salt and pepper, with black markings across her shoulders and down her back. Her chest was gray, her legs and ears tawny-brown, and she had a black tip to her tail.

After she had fed her newborn babies and they were sleeping at her side, she heard a soft scuffling at the entrance to the den. Moments later, Nell's father shouldered his way through the narrow tunnel. He was bigger than his mate and had more silver in his coat. In his jaws he carried a freshly killed rabbit.

While Nell's mother tore the rabbit apart and ate it, he sniffed the pups and gave each one a lick. Until the babies were weaned, it was his duty to bring food to their mother and to care for them during the short periods she was away from the den.

The den was on a slope bordering an overgrown field. It had been the home of a fox before it was taken over by Nell's parents. The original den had been too small for a coyote family, so Nell's mother had enlarged the tunnel and the single underground chamber. She began this job at the entrance, digging furiously with her forepaws and clearing with her hind feet. Eventually she disappeared underground, but earth continued to spurt from the hole.

When she was finished, the entrance was surrounded by a pile of sandy loam. The light color of the soil made it easy for any passerby to spot the den. Even a human.

◆

A week after Nell was born, two teenaged boys were out practicing with a .22 rifle. They used tin cans as targets, but soon became bored. Then a flock of crows flew by, and they decided to try to shoot one. As they stalked these wary black birds, they came to a field next to the one where Nell lived. Carefully they scanned the surrounding trees, but found no crows. However, on the far side of the field they saw a woodchuck.

Rifle at the ready, they crept toward the animal sitting by its burrow. They didn't get very far before the woodchuck also spied them. With a shrill whistle of alarm, it bolted down its hole.

"He's sure to come out again," said the older boy. "We'll hide over there and shoot him when his head pops up."

The teenagers hid themselves in a drainage ditch. From time to time, one of them would peep over the edge to see if the woodchuck had come out. The shadows gradually lengthened. Still the woodchuck did not appear.

Just as they were about to give up, one of the boys noticed something move at the edge of the field.

Nudging his friend, he whispered, "Look over there!"

It was Nell's father returning to the den with food for his mate. Because the boys stayed still and were downwind of him, the coyote didn't see or smell them. Calmly he trotted out into the open. Suddenly he stopped in mid-stride, sensing danger.

The boys were astonished to see the coyote standing in front of them. For the space of a heartbeat no one moved. Then one of the boys grabbed the rifle, flung it to his shoulder and fired. He was so excited that he didn't aim, and the bullet went wide, harmlessly kicking up a clod of earth. There was no chance for a second shot. At the crack of the rifle, the coyote vanished.

Jumping to their feet, the boys ran to the spot where the animal had disappeared. They studied the ground for signs of blood, but there were none. Then they tried to track him by following his footprints. Aside from scuff marks in the dirt where the coyote had whirled away at the shot, there were no tracks.

By now the sun was low on the horizon. The teenagers gave up their search and started home. Instead of retracing their steps, they took a shortcut through the next field. The path they chose led them right past the coyote den.

"Hey! What's this?"

"Must be where that coyote lives."

"Do you think the critter's in there?"

"Put your head in the hole and see."

"Think I'm crazy? You put your head in the hole!"

"Okay, if you're chicken, I'll do it myself."

The older boy got down on his knees and looked into the entrance. He could see a little way, but then the tunnel made a bend. Edging forward, he put his head into the hole.

Inside the den, Nell's mother drew her body more closely around her sleeping babies. She had heard the humans coming, and every word they had spoken. Her heart thumped, and she breathed in shallow gasps. She was terrified. But she would defend her babies with her life.

When the light was blotted out in the tunnel by the intruder, she bared her teeth and snarled a deep-throated warning.

The boy leapt back from the hole.

"It's in there!" he cried.

"Let's dig it out."

"We don't have anything to dig with, stupid! Besides, it's getting dark. We'll have to come back tomorrow." The older boy thought for a moment. "But before we go, we'll block the hole so it can't get away."

After looking around, they selected a fallen tree to block the entrance. The tree was too heavy to lift, so they dragged it to the den.

Grunting with effort, they pulled the trunk over the hole. Then, with two large rocks, they wedged the tree in place.

As they walked away, the older teenager said, "Maybe we'll get a bounty for that coyote."

"What's a bounty?" asked his friend.

"It's money the government pays to kill pests like coyotes."

"If there's a whole family in that den, will they pay us for the young ones, too?"

"Maybe. I guess it depends how big they are…" Their voices faded away in the dusk.

◆

When Nell's mother was sure the humans had gone, she detached herself from her babies. Stepping carefully around the pups, she entered another tunnel at the back of the chamber. This was an escape passage that came out behind the den under the roots of a tree. She emerged from it like a shadow and crept to the top of the bank. There she listened, sniffed the wind and scanned the dark underbrush for danger.

When the mother coyote was satisfied that it was safe, she pointed her muzzle to the sky and barked twice. *Woof! Woof!* After a pause, she barked softly again. Then she waited.

Before long, her mate stepped into the little clearing. Nose to nose, with wagging tails, the coyotes greeted each other.

Nell's mother went back into the den. A minute or so later, she emerged with one of the pups in her mouth. Nell's father entered the den and came out with another baby. Carrying their precious burdens with care, the coyotes set off through the night. Their destination was another den that had been prepared for just such an emergency. It was located among boulders at the base of a cliff, and had once been the home of a porcupine.

Nell was the last of the five babies to be moved to the new den. Although her mother had forty-two sharp teeth and jaws powerful enough to crush the leg bone of a deer, she was so gentle that Nell slept throughout the journey.

By dawn the coyote family was in its new home. Because the entrance to this den was a crevice among the boulders, and there was no freshly dug earth to be seen, it was well hidden. A few hours later, the coyotes heard humans talking at the old den, and the ring of a shovel against stone. Instantly alert, with ears erect, they tuned into the sounds of danger.

After a time, however, they relaxed. Nell's mother put her nose between her paws and closed her yellow eyes.

For now, the family was safe.

CHAPTER 2

Leaving the Den

NELL'S eyes opened ten days after she was born. During this period her weight had doubled, and her face had become more pointed. The pups' coats had turned brownish-gray with a dark stripe down the back. Except for Nell, whose fine wooly coat was charcoal-gray.

The most important change was being able to see. This opened a whole new world for Nell. Now she could move around the earth floor of the den wherever she pleased. She could also wrestle and play with her litter mates. But most often, because she was still very young, she slept and played with her mother.

Mother coyote was good-natured and let the pups nip at her ears and ruff, and even her tail. When they became too much for her, she simply moved away.

About the third week the pups grew baby teeth. These teeth, though small, were needle-sharp. From this point on, when the pups got too rough, their mother would warn them by baring her fangs. Or she would growl at them. If one of the pups was very naughty, she would roll him on his back and pin him down with a paw on his tummy.

Nell peeked out of the den for the first time when she was three weeks old. After the darkness, it was amazingly bright, and she had to squint her eyes to see. It was also frightening, and after a few minutes she crept back into the den.

For the next little while, life continued much as usual. Nell played with her brothers and sister and stayed close to her mother. But day by day the pups were becoming more active, and more curious. From time to time Nell would stray to the entrance of the den to look outside. Thor, her big brother, even took several steps away from the den while Nell watched from the entrance. Then he lost his nerve and hurried back to safety.

A week later, Nell and Thor went outside together. Although they were scared, being together gave them courage. Sniffing at stones, flowers and blades of grass, they wandered away from the den. They didn't go very far but were soon out of sight of their mother.

Soaring high above, a bald eagle scanned the ground for something to eat. Its eyes, like binoculars, spotted the two baby coyotes. Gracefully the eagle swung in an arc, spilled air from its wings and spiraled down to a dead elm tree. Nell and Thor looked up when the huge bird with its black body and white head landed above them. Gripping the branch with curved talons, the eagle studied the two plump morsels below. Clicking its yellow beak, it thought about which one to grab.

Just then, Nell's mother appeared. Taking in the scene, she snarled at the eagle and raced to the side of her babies. The eagle and the coyote glared at each other. Then, admitting defeat, the eagle lifted from the branch and flapped slowly away.

Nell and Thor didn't understand what had happened, but they knew their mother was angry with them for leaving her side. With their mother growling at their heels, they scampered back to the den.

The pups were weaned when they were five weeks old. The change from their mother's milk to solid food was made gradually. To begin with, their mother chewed up pieces of meat for them, but also fed them her milk. After about ten days, they ate only solid food. Whenever they were hungry (which was most of the time) they would nudge their mother's muzzle or lick her lips, hoping for a chewed-up mouse or a piece of ground rabbit.

By June it was clear that Thor, Nell's big brother, was the boss of the litter. He was the strongest, the boldest, and he always won the play fights. Nell was smaller than her other two brothers, Ruff and Digger, but she held her own because she was quicker than they were. So, Nell ranked next to Thor. Then came Ruff and Digger. At the bottom was Lottie, the other female in the litter. Lottie was the smallest and the most timid in the family.

The coyote family moved out of the den at the end of June. Their new home was a mixed stand of young spruce and fir trees. These low evergreens screened the pups from view, sheltered them from the rain and provided shade during the hottest days. There was also plenty to eat. In the thick grass beneath the trees lived countless mice and voles. And there were lots of berries around the fringes of the grove. Both coyote parents looked after and played with the little ones.

Nell learned to hunt here. One of her favorite games in the den had been to creep up and then pounce on one of her litter mates. The trick was to surprise your opponent. Now she tried out her skills on a variety of small creatures.

Nell's first attempts to stalk and kill were rarely successful. Beetles were quite easy. Usually she could pounce on them before they got away. Butterflies looked easy, sitting so bright and still, but often floated out of reach at the last moment. Crickets were small and frustrating. They were not only hard to see, but just as she pounced, the cricket would jump to the side. The same could be said for little spotted frogs. Mice were the most difficult of all because they were so quick. Moles and voles were slower and quite often got caught.

The pups learned the proper way to catch a mouse from their father. He showed them how to do it over and over again. First he moved very quietly with his nose to the ground. When he smelled a mouse, he would slowly move his head from side to side to pinpoint its location. Quick as a flash, he would pounce with his paws together to trap the mouse. Then he would grab it in his mouth, bite it and throw it in the air. Sometimes he would let the dead mouse fall to the ground, and the pups would race for it. But if he was hungry, he would catch it in midair and swallow it in one swift gulp.

Birds, unless they were fledglings, were impossible for the pups to catch. Once they came upon a mother grouse with chicks. At the approach of the young coyotes, the mother grouse cheeped a warning to her babies. Instantly the mottled-brown chicks scurried for cover. Then the mother grouse, pretending she had a broken wing, showed herself to the coyotes. Seeing her slowly dragging her wing, they rushed after her. To their surprise she managed to stay just of reach. The chase continued for some time. When she had led the coyotes a safe distance from her family, the grouse gave up her pretence of being injured. With a roar of wings, she rocketed away through the trees.

Beginning in August, the pups were left alone for much of the day. When either parent returned, each would stop and give a howl to let the pups know they were coming. The pups would howl back their greeting with a series of excited barks, yips and high-pitched shrieks. Being left alone for hours wasn't much fun, but it taught the young ones to be independent.

It was also in August that their parents introduced them to serious hunting. From then on the pups accompanied their mother and father on their regular hunts. These hunts usually took place after dusk or at dawn. The first outings were quite brief, but gradually the amount of time and the distances covered were increased.

Learning to hunt was an important part of growing up. Soon, the young ones would be on their own.

CHAPTER 3

Blueberry Time

B Y the beginning of August, Nell no longer looked like a puppy. The young coyotes resembled their parents, but they were smaller. Nell was the only one who was different. Her coat was chocolate-brown shading to black, with shiny guard hairs. From a distance, she looked black. This dark coloring is rare among Eastern coyotes.

When their parents were absent, the young often went off on their own. One afternoon in August, Nell and her brother Thor left the sheltering evergreens to find something to eat. Eventually they came upon an open area carpeted with wild blueberries, a favorite coyote delicacy.

The two young coyotes went from bush to bush, raking berries off the branches with their teeth. As they did so, they slowly wandered apart. While bees droned and the sun warmed their coats, they gorged until the juice stained their tongues blue. Absorbed in their feast, they lost track of each other.

What Nell and Thor didn't know was that someone else was in the blueberry patch. Out of sight behind a clump of willows, a black bear and her young cub were also eating berries. Thor and Nell were upwind of the bears and couldn't smell them. Unaware of the danger, Thor worked his way between the mother bear and her cub.

The mother bear, being shortsighted, didn't notice Thor's gray form in the bushes until she caught a whiff of his scent. Alarmed, she looked around to locate the coyote. Then she rose on her hind feet. Thor saw the huge animal tower above him. At the same time, the bear caught sight of the coyote and let out a growl of rage.

Nell, who was off to the side, heard the bear roar. At a glance she saw the terrible danger. Jumping from behind the bush, she barked sharply. The bear, who had been about to attack Thor, whirled on Nell. Confused by the appearance of a second threat to her cub, the powerful beast hesitated for a moment. Thor seized his opportunity and bolted into the undergrowth. Nell fled in a different direction.

Uncertain which coyote to chase, the bear only went a few steps before returning to her cub. The cub got a cuff for straying. Then the two went back to eating berries. Meanwhile, Nell ran like the wind, sure that the bear was on her heels.

After a time, Nell came to a corn field. With a quick glance over her shoulder, she disappeared into the corn. Hidden by the tall stalks, she followed a row deep into the field. Then she doubled back on her trail and lay down to wait. The breeze rustled the papery leaves, and she heard the caw of a distant crow. Otherwise, nothing stirred. The bear hadn't followed her.

But what about Thor? Nell didn't know where he was, and she wasn't even sure of her own position.

There was only one thing to do. Screened by the green stalks, she raised her muzzle and howled. Very faintly, she heard an answering howl.

It was Thor! Nell set off at a lope in his direction. At the same time, Thor started toward his sister.

Minutes later, Nell came upon Thor's trail.

She followed it and soon saw her brother through the trees. The two coyotes met with wagging tails and sniffs of greeting. Then, from a far-off hill, they heard the yips and howls of the family pack. With a sense of relief, they headed for the familiar sounds. It had been an exciting day. ◆

As August unfolded into September, the bond between the adult coyotes and their young continued to weaken. This was normal, for Nature sees to it that young coyotes leave their parents in the autumn or early winter. One of the reasons is that the parents' territory—the area they hunt in—may not have enough food to feed the young when they are fully grown.

Not all the pups, however, leave their parents. Some stay until the following autumn, or even longer. Pups who stay with their parents help to raise the next litter. They act as caring "uncles" and "aunts."

Before leaving for good, the young coyotes explored the countryside. These trips often lasted overnight, and sometimes longer. Nell, with her brothers Thor and Ruff, went exploring just after Labor Day. They were away for three days.

The first afternoon, they reached a thickly forested valley. A muddy river trickled through it. Except to the north, where they had come from, they were surrounded by mixed farmland. Some of the fields were overgrown with alders, poplar trees and small evergreens. These neglected fields were home to snowshoe hares and countless little four-footed creatures. Fruit was also plentiful—dark chokecherries, wild apples and scarlet hawthorn berries. And there was a field of corn nearby. Resting in the long grass before sunset on their first evening, the three coyotes decided to make the valley their base.

Although game was plentiful, only about one in ten of their chases was successful. Sometimes, what they caught turned out to be a surprise. Like the time Thor caught a short-tailed shrew.

It was dark when Thor stalked and pinned what he thought was a mouse. It was charcoal-gray with a pointy nose and little pink feet. Thor speared his victim with his paws, just as his father had taught him, and crunched it in his jaws to kill it. The taste was awful! Ruff picked up the dead animal, but spat it out, too.

Then Nell did the same thing. After examining the shrew thoroughly, they left it and continued their hunt. They wouldn't forget the musky odor of the short-tailed shrew. Nor would they try to eat one again.

The coyotes started for home at sunset on the third day. At the head of the valley, they came to a bridge. A dirt road led north, and they decided to follow it.

As they loped along the darkened road, they heard the sound of a motor. Then the vehicle's lights swept the trees on either side of them. A truck was coming! Seconds later, the three coyotes were caught in the glare of the headlights.

The driver was a deer hunter who hated coyotes (because some coyotes also kill deer). As soon as he saw the fleeing animals, he stepped on the gas. This was his chance to kill a coyote.

Running flat out, Nell, Thor and Ruff clung to the edge of the road. They should have left the road but they were panic-stricken. As the truck drew closer, the young coyotes were deafened by its roar.

When the truck came abreast, the driver turned the wheel sharply to run over them.

Instead, he lost control of his vehicle, which veered off the road and ended up in the ditch. Nell, Thor and Ruff left the gravel and escaped into the bush.

This experience taught them two valuable lessons. Roads were dangerous, and humans were to be feared.

Aside from the near-disaster on the road, the coyotes' trip had been a success. They had survived on their own for three days. They had also sharpened their hunting skills, and thanks to abundant fruit and corn, they had eaten well. This gave them confidence, which they would need. For all three were about to leave home for good.

CHAPTER 4

The Forest Fire

NELL left her parents' home in October, the time of scarlet and gold. Thor, her favorite brother, went with her. Ruff and Digger left a few days apart in November, when the trees were bare. Lottie, the smallest and most timid, stayed with her parents. She would help to raise the next litter and leave home the following year.

Coyotes' lives are always at risk. But leaving home is perhaps the time of greatest peril. Ruff was shot by a deer hunter a week after he went out on his own. Digger was killed by a trapper on Christmas Eve.

When Nell and Thor left that October morning, dawn was a pink glow on the horizon. It was so cold they could see their breath. Delicately picking their way, they headed for the valley they had visited with Ruff. Two lines of dark prints in the frost-whitened grass marked their trail.

Along the route, somber evergreens contrasted with stands of brilliant hardwoods. As the coyotes passed beneath the hardwood trees, the breeze spilled red and yellow leaves upon them. Underfoot, the path changed from granite outcroppings to carpets of pine needles and fallen leaves.

Nell and Thor kept up a steady pace. Late in the afternoon, when the sun was beginning to lose its warmth, they entered the forested valley. They were tired and hungry, for it had been a long day. But this was not their final destination. Before first light they were on the move again, following the valley south.

During the morning they passed farms where they had to watch out for humans. Once, crossing a pasture, they were forced to crawl on their bellies to avoid being seen by a farmer. As it was, the farmer's dog did spot them and barked wildly, but no one paid any attention. Then the valley reverted to forest, and they were able to continue in safety.

Around noon they came to a large lake. Here they rested.

From the bank, Nell and Thor saw a red canoe coming up the lake. A man paddled in the stern, a woman paddled in the bow, and two children sat amidships on the floor of the canoe. All four members of the family wore yellow life vests. The two coyotes watched the canoe draw abreast of them and then continue up the lake. After it passed out of sight, the coyotes relaxed and drifted into a light sleep.

◆

Twenty minutes later, the family landed on the same side of the lake, upwind from the coyotes. After they pulled the canoe up on the sand, they built a fire and cooked hot dogs for lunch. The wind kept increasing, and the adults began to worry about getting back before the lake became too rough. As soon as the meal was finished, they decided to go. They were in such a hurry that they packed their plates and cups without washing them. And, to save time while he readied the canoe, the father sent his children to put a final pail of water on the campfire, rather than doing it himself.

Sarah and Tim, who were aged seven and nine, filled the pail in the lake and went back up the path to the campfire. When they arrived, they saw that their father had drenched the center of the fire. Their job was to check for smoldering embers around the edges and make sure they were out. Tim bent over to study the ashes.

At that moment Sarah called in alarm.

"Tim! There's something behind that bush!"

"Where?"

"Over there!"

As they watched, a gust of wind shook the bush.

"See, it's moving again. Maybe it's a bear!" cried Sarah.

Keeping his eyes on the bush, Tim quickly dumped the pail of water on the fire.

"Let's go!" he shouted.

The two ran back down the path as fast as they could. Their parents, anxious to get away, hastily settled the children in the canoe and pushed off. As they paddled down the lake, squalls of wind slapped the stern and rocked the canoe.

The wind also dislodged an ember under one of the rocks at the campfire, turning it from gray to glowing red. The ember rolled into a little pile of dead leaves, which burst into flame. Within minutes, the campsite was ablaze.

◆

Nell and Thor saw the canoe pass by hugging the shoreline. Soon after, they smelled a strange odor. It was borne on the wind, and grew stronger. Muzzles pointed into the breeze, black nostrils quivering, they tried to identify the smell.

In the distance, they heard a crackling sound. This too was a mystery. Instinct told them to flee, but curiosity got the better of them. With a sense of unease, they decided to follow their noses and find out what was happening.

Ahead, a pall of smoke darkened the sky. The acrid smell became intense, and the crackling sounds grew louder. When they reached the top of the ridge, they were met by a blast of hot air. In front was a wall of flames capped by billowing clouds of smoke.

For a minute they simply stared. They had never seen fire before. As they stood, the fire continued to advance, gobbling everything before it. Close by, a pine tree exploded into a gigantic torch. The sight of the tree snapped

the coyotes out of their trance. Terror-stricken, they ran back to the valley.

At first they thought they'd escaped. But moments later the fire was upon them again—roaring, felling trees and blotting out the landscape. With frightening speed the fire boxed in the coyotes on three sides. Then the flames curved around behind them. They were trapped!

Through the smoke, flying embers and falling branches, the coyotes saw the lake. But to get there meant crossing a swath of burning forest. They had no choice. The fire was gaining strength on all sides.

Nell and Thor made a dash for it. Seconds later a tree crashed down between them in a shower of sparks, and they lost contact with each other. Deafened by the roar and nearly blinded by the smoke, they somehow managed to make it to the lake. Sticking to the water's edge, they worked their way down the lake to a large marsh.

Safely out of reach of the flames, they stumbled and swam to the middle of the marsh. Here they dragged themselves up on a muskrat house. Exhausted, they lay panting on the pile of mud and reeds. Later they groomed their singed fur and burned paws with their tongues.

That evening an autumn storm drowned the fire. When the rain ended the next morning, the countryside no longer reflected the colors of an artist's palette. Instead, Nell and Thor saw a wasteland of blackened trees, charred stumps and steaming ashes.

There was no point in staying. They would have to move on.

CHAPTER 5

Starboot

T HE fire forced Nell and Thor to detour west toward Algonquin Park. Progress was slow. Their paws were still sore from being burned, making it more difficult for them to stalk and catch game. For the first few days they ate windfall apples and corn left by the harvesters.

As they journeyed on, the country changed from farmland to rock, scrub bush and twisted pines. This barren land offered little to eat, and Nell was constantly hungry. Rabbits were scarce, which meant she had to spend a lot of energy catching small animals like mice and moles to make a meal. Sometimes she got so hungry she ate dead grass to ease the pain in her stomach.

At dusk one evening, Nell and Thor came upon a porcupine. For a coyote, a porcupine can provide a delicious meal, because its flesh is sweet and it has a thick layer of fat in the autumn. But getting that meal can be a dangerous challenge.

A porcupine's head, back, sides and tail are covered with thousands of sharp quills. These quills are like needles, and they have tiny barbs. The barbs not only make the quills difficult to pull out, but cause them to work deeper into the flesh. Although a porcupine can't throw its quills, it can loosen them so they penetrate at the slightest touch. The only places a porcupine doesn't have quills are its face and stomach.

Nell and Thor came upon the porcupine as it was shuffling along the ground toward a hemlock tree. When it caught the scent of the coyotes, it broke into a shambling run. Thor dashed between the porcupine and the hemlock while Nell stayed behind to prevent it from escaping up another tree.

Like a dark bundle of hay with beady black eyes, the cornered porcupine stared at the coyotes. Then, quills raised, it turned its back to them. Nell and Thor attacked. The scene resembled a wild dance, with the coyotes jumping back and forth to threaten the porcupine. Whenever a coyote came too close, the porcupine lashed its tail. Both Nell and Thor were nearly clubbed, which could have blinded them.

The minutes went by, and the porcupine slowly began to tire. Eventually, when Nell darted in and the porcupine was slow to react, Thor saw his chance. Springing from the darkness, he grabbed the porcupine by its face. With a crunch of his powerful jaws, he flipped the animal onto its back, exposing its belly. Seconds later the coyotes were feasting on their victim. It was their first good meal in a week.

Near the end of October it snowed. Nell had never seen snow before, and the sight of white flakes drifting from the sky took her by surprise. At first she just watched it fall, muffling the sounds of the forest. Then she sniffed the snow and tasted the icy flakes, which made her tongue tingle. Gingerly she tiptoed through the snow to see if it held any danger. When she and Thor were satisfied that it contained no threat, they frolicked and rolled about, playing like pups.

Although it was autumn, the snow lasted for several days. It came at a bad time for snowshoe hares, who hadn't completed their color change to winter white. Their patchy brown coats stood out against the snow, making them easy to spot. As well, the snow left the footprints of passing animals and even the delicate tracks of grouse. These telltale signs helped Nell and Thor find their quarry. They also revealed that the two coyotes weren't the only large predators in the area.

A single set of tracks, similar to theirs but twice as big, told them that their large cousin, the gray wolf, was nearby. From the sharpness of the imprint, the wolf had come by within the past few hours.

That evening Nell heard a long, drawn-out wail—the howl of a wolf. The lone cry was answered by a pack of wolves in the distance. These eerie calls made Nell tremble with fear, for if the wolves caught them, they would kill them. But the coyotes had to wait until the wolves were closer so they would know which way to flee.

Straining their eyes and ears, Nell and Thor tried to locate the pack. Finally, when the moon was high, they saw a line of seven shadows bounding across the snow. Their vantage point was upwind of the wolves, which were chasing a deer. The coyotes watched the wolves pass, waited until they could no longer hear them, and then set off in the opposite direction. Moving at a steady lope, Nell and Thor didn't stop until mid-morning of the following day. By then they were well clear of their enemies.

Their flight had taken them farther south, to farmland mixed with forest. Food was a little more plentiful, but still scarce.

Returning after dawn from a hunt, Nell and Thor came upon an animal that looked like a big gray cat with a ringed tail and a black mask. The raccoon didn't run at their approach. It tried to get away, but something held its front paw. Nell and Thor moved closer for a better look. The raccoon was caught in the jaws of a steel trap chained to a buried stake. From the blood on the snow and the torn vegetation, the animal had been there for hours, struggling to free itself.

Just then, the coyotes heard a motor approaching. Quickly they retreated to a grove of cedar trees. Moments later the vehicle came into view, driven by a man wearing heavy clothes and an orange hat.

Lying on her belly under the skirts of a cedar tree, Nell watched as the man stopped his machine by the raccoon. Carrying a thick hardwood stick, he strode toward the trapped animal, which tried to hide, but was held by the chain. With a grunt, the man brought down the club on the raccoon's head. Stepping closer, the trapper hit the animal three more times. Then he released the spring of the trap and threw the dead raccoon into the back of his vehicle.

Just as he was about to leave, he noticed the coyotes' footprints. Grabbing his rifle from a case on the back of his vehicle, he started toward the trees.

Nell and Thor, who had watched the man's every move, bolted from their hiding place. The trapper only caught a glimpse of Thor, but he got a good look at Nell.

Under his breath he said, "I'll get those coyotes. I'll sell the gray pelt, but the hide of the black one will go on my wall."

That night, Nell and Thor returned to where the trapper had caught the raccoon. The man's footprints were clearly printed in the snow—a large boot with a star design on the heel. The two coyotes sniffed the area, memo-rizing the scent of the human and the shape of his print.

Starboot was a killer. They would have to watch out for him.

CHAPTER 6

The Snare

A FTER their encounter with Starboot, Nell and Thor traveled south throughout the night. When morning came, they thought they were out of danger, not realizing that Starboot's trapline included this area as well.

The next day a warm front passed through, bringing with it high winds and rain, which melted the snow. During the storm, rabbits and other small animals holed up in their dens and burrows, so Nell and Thor went hungry. That night the temperature fell. The sky cleared, and the stars came out. Before dawn, the two coyotes set off to find their breakfast.

They stalked a snowshoe hare and flushed a ruffed grouse but weren't able to catch either of them. By sunup they still hadn't had anything to eat. On their way back they followed the bank of a stream. Tired, with tails held low, they trudged along until they came to a place where the water had been dammed to form a pond. Sensing game, they paused to sniff the breeze.

It was then that Nell saw the beavers. One was swimming in the pond. Another was working on the lodge—an untidy mound of mud and sticks in the center of the dam. A third was on land, dragging a poplar branch to the water's edge.

Nell took a step forward. As she did so, her movement caught the eye of the swimming beaver.

Whack! Slapping the water with its broad tail, the beaver dove beneath the surface. At his warning signal, the other two beavers plunged into the pond and disappeared. By the time the ripples had faded, all three beavers were safely in their lodge.

Nell and Thor had encountered beavers before and knew they couldn't pursue them. The entrance to the beaver lodge was under water, and its walls were as thick as a fortress. But they also knew that if they waited, the beavers would eventually come out.

A beaver is wonderfully agile in the water but quite clumsy on land. For this reason, the coyotes chose the path between the poplars and the pond for their ambush. Quietly taking up positions on either side of the path, they lay down to wait.

Just before sunset, a sleek head popped out of the water by the lodge. The beaver looked around for several minutes, then sank from sight. A little while later two heads appeared, and one of the beavers climbed onto the lodge.

The stars were out when a beaver finally came up the path, bound for the poplars. Not moving a muscle, Nell watched it through half-closed eyes. When it came between them, both coyotes sprang. Although the beaver weighed almost as much as Nell, the fight was over in seconds. Nell and Thor gorged until they could eat no more.

They returned to their kill the next day. In the meantime, ravens, jays, foxes and other wild creatures had fed on the carcass, and only scraps were left. A faint footprint in the mud showed that there had also been another visitor. Starboot. Intent on getting something to eat, neither Nell nor Thor noticed this ominous sign.

The coyotes continued their hunt. A few

minutes downstream, they rounded a bend and came upon a white-tailed deer. The yearling buck was drinking at the edge of a backwater.

Both Nell and Thor stopped in mid-stride and sank to the ground. The deer caught a glimpse of their movement and brought his head up. Ears erect, white-edged tail flicking from side to side, the young buck stared in the coyotes' direction. Nervously stamping his hooves, he approached a few steps closer to get a better look. Then he caught a whiff of their scent. Coyotes! With a loud snort, the deer bounded away into the dark.

Nell and Thor chased after him, but the buck easily kept ahead of them. The coyotes then changed their tactics. Instead of trying to outrun the deer, they hung back and simply kept him in sight. The deer soon became less frightened, slowed his pace and made a wide circle back toward the stream. As soon as he did this, Nell and Thor split up. Nell followed the deer while Thor doubled back to the stream.

The buck, seeing Nell far behind him, gradually worked his way toward a cedar swamp bordering the stream. Thor was lying in wait at the edge of the cedars.

The deer was taken off guard when Thor leapt from the underbrush. Thor hit the buck with his full force and clamped his teeth on the animal's neck. The deer sprang to the side and bolted off through the trees. Thor was flung about like a rag doll, but he kept his grip.

The struggle raged through the cedars for some minutes. Eventually the crushing effect of Thor's teeth on the deer's throat took its toll. The buck sank to his knees. Nell moved in to help Thor make the kill. Together they ripped the buck open and fed until they were covered with blood to their eyes. Then, sated with red meat, they lay down and slept.

They returned to the kill the next evening. Although other forest dwellers had also fed on the remains of the buck, there was plenty left. Indeed, there was enough meat on the carcass to make it worthwhile for them to return again.

◆

Starboot walked around the dead deer, studying it from every angle. At one point he got down on one knee to check the footprints by the carcass. The prints confirmed that two coy-

otes had been there—they'd probably killed the deer—and it was likely that one of them was the black coyote.

Starboot scratched the stubble on his chin, wondering which trap to use. From his bag he took a length of woven steel cable shaped like a noose, with a locking device. Starboot opened the noose to the size of a basketball. Then he suspended the loop between two cedar trees to block the path leading to the dead deer. Carefully, he adjusted the noose so that it hung above the ground at the height of a coyote's head. The snare—which was nearly invisible—was anchored by fine steel cable to the trunk of a large cedar tree.

Before he left, Starboot straightened up the surrounding vegetation and swept away his tracks with a cedar branch. All was now in readiness for the coyotes.

◆

That evening, Thor led the way through the cedar swamp. Nell was a few paces behind him. It was one of the few times they knew where to find their next meal, and they were looking forward to it.

Suddenly, Thor stopped in the narrow path,

and Nell almost ran into him. Thor tried to go ahead, but he could not. Then he tried to back up, but he couldn't do that, either. Something was wrong. He moved to the side and for a moment seemed to break free. But after a few steps he was jerked up short.

Something was around his neck! And every time he pulled against it, the noose got tighter.

Thor was in deadly danger, and Nell didn't know what to do. He was panting for breath, so she licked his muzzle to comfort him. But that wasn't much help. Then she backed away to give him room to escape. Again and again he moved to the side and, thinking he had broken free, ran until he hit the end of the steel cable. Each time he was upended, the noose tightened another notch.

Thor fought the snare for hours, but as the night wore on, his struggles gradually became weaker. Just before dawn, he died of strangulation.

Nell, who had watched helplessly all night, went up to her brother and sniffed his still form. When he didn't respond, she whimpered and turned away. A few minutes later, she lifted her nose to the sky and let out a series of howls, telling the stars of her grief.

Nell stayed by Thor even after the sun came up. Sometime during the morning she heard a vehicle approaching. It was Starboot. The trapper went up to Thor and looked at him for a long minute. Rifle in hand, he prodded the coyote with his boot to make sure he was dead. Then he unfastened the snare and held Thor up by the hind feet to admire his pelt.

It was then that Starboot sensed that he was being watched. Slowly turning around, he scanned the dark cedars. He didn't see Nell, but he knew she was there.

"I'll get you next, you black devil," he muttered.

CHAPTER 7

Alone

AFTER Thor was killed, Nell moved on. It was too dangerous to stay in the same vicinity as Starboot. The first few weeks on her own were very lonely. Nell lost weight and her coat lost its sheen.

Without Thor as her partner, hunting was much more difficult. To add to her problems, winter had set in. The bone-chilling temperatures meant that she needed more to eat to keep warm.

Hares were hard to see because their white winter coats blended perfectly with their surroundings. And when she located a hare by scent, it ran so fast and turned so sharply that it usually got away. Small rodents—mice, moles and voles—now spent most of their time safely hidden in tunnels under the snow. Even ruffed grouse sometimes burrowed under the icy blanket. The few times Nell came upon the breathing hole of a grouse and tried to dig it out, it escaped in a shower of snow.

Nell managed to survive—by hunting from dusk till dawn—but she was constantly hungry. As the cold increased, so did her hunger. At the end of January the temperature plummeted, frozen trees cracked like pistol shots, and snow lay deep in the forest.

Late one afternoon Nell heard the hollow croak of a raven. Looking up, she saw its black form against the pale sky. The raven, flying toward a nearby lake, gave another low croak. Nell recognized the cries as a feeding call.

Changing direction, Nell followed the raven. When she reached the fringe of trees at the edge of the lake, she stopped. Out on the ice several ravens and crows were eating something. She couldn't see what it was, so she moved downwind to see if she could smell it. When she tasted the breeze, it wafted the delicious scent of deer meat to her.

◆

On the other side of the lake, two men on a snowmobile hid among the trees. The driver watched the ice through a pair of binoculars, while the other man cradled a high-powered rifle in his arms. They had been there since noon, hoping to get a shot at the wolves that had killed the deer.

The man with the binoculars suddenly said, "There's a wolf heading for the carcass!" A moment later he changed his mind. "Maybe it's not a wolf. It's too small. Could be a black dog."

His partner didn't reply. The man with the binoculars took another look and started the snowmobile.

"I think it's a coyote!" he exclaimed.

His partner levered a bullet into the chamber of the rifle.

"Let's go!"

◆

Nell was reluctant to leave the safety of the trees. She knew that if she went out on the lake she could be seen by enemies—both wolves and humans—and she would have no protective cover. On the other hand, she was desperately hungry.

While she wrestled with the problem, two more ravens flew down to the remains. The sight of these wary birds flocking to the kill made up her mind. If it was safe enough for them, it must be safe enough for her.

Cautiously she stepped from the trees and started across the ice.

Just as she reached the deer carcass, she heard a sound that made her heart stop. On the other side of the lake a snowmobile burst from the trees. Engine roaring, it came toward her with frightening speed. Terrified, Nell turned and ran for the opposite shore.

Patches of slick ice slowed her flight, and the snowmobile kept getting closer. Shots rang out. Nell saw spurts of snow on either side of her. One bullet nicked the top of her ear, but she didn't feel it. Then, just before she made it to safety, the snowmobile stopped. The rifleman took deliberate aim.

Bang!

Nell was knocked over by the force of the bullet. Dazed, she lay still for several seconds.

Thinking they had made a kill, the men started toward her. The sound of the engine jerked Nell to her senses, and she jumped up. Instantly her hind leg gave way and she fell over. With a great effort she managed to stand on three legs and hobble into the woods.

By the time the men arrived, Nell had disappeared into the dense mass of evergreens. They followed her trail in the snow to the edge of a cliff, but they couldn't figure out which direction she had taken after that. The sun had melted the snow along the sheltered base of the cliff, and Nell had run along the bare rocks, leaving no tracks.

Disgusted, the men returned to where they'd shot Nell. After looking at the blood and hairs marking the spot where she'd fallen, they decided they had mortally wounded her, and she had staggered off to die. Because the light was fading, there was no point in following now. Tomorrow at first light they would come back and track her down.

While the men were talking, Nell was making her escape. She had fallen heavily going over the cliff, and her left hind leg was numb, but she could run quite well on three legs. Driven by fear, she kept on going for nearly six hours. Then, exhausted, she crept under a spruce tree to rest and lick her wounds.

She had been lucky. The bullet had passed through the back of her thigh and out the other side, narrowly missing a main artery and the bone. Her right ear had a small nick on the outer edge, but had stopped bleeding. Although her leg was throbbing painfully, it would heal. Around midnight it began to snow. Nell drifted into an uneasy sleep.

A shaft of sunlight on her nose woke her the next morning. Her leg was very sore and stiff, and she stretched painfully. Looking out from under the tree, she saw that a thick layer of snow had erased her tracks. The sight of the snow lifted her spirits, for she knew the humans couldn't follow her now. For the time being she was safe, but she was weak with hunger.

Limping along on three legs, she scented a grouse under the snow. Slowly and carefully she approached the air hole. When she pounced, her bad leg gave way, and she lost her balance. The grouse exploded from the snow and flew off. A second later it crashed into a maple tree and fell to the ground in a cloud of brown feathers. Nell was upon it in an instant.

For a change, Fate had been kind. It was a good sign.

CHAPTER 8

Turning the Tables

NELL stayed in the area for three weeks. By then her wounds had healed, leaving her with a tiny patch of white fur where the bullet had pierced her leg, and a notch in her ear. As her strength returned, she became increasingly restless and lonely. At the end of February she resumed her search for a home and a mate.

She headed south because she was hemmed in on both sides by human settlements. The first obstacle she encountered was the broad, partly frozen Severn River.

Nell prowled the bank looking for a place to cross on the sun-rotted ice. Several times she ventured out on the frozen surface but changed her mind. Eventually she selected a spot above an open stretch and started across.

Slipping and sliding, she made slow progress. When she reached the middle, the ice started to creak. Alarmed by the sound,

Nell turned to go back. Just as she did so, a crack appeared in the ice. The crack widened and a film of water seeped from it. A moment later Nell felt the surface shift beneath her feet. Suddenly, the ice gave way.

Nell was stunned by the cold water. Before she could recover, she was pulled under the ice. Just when she thought her lungs would burst, she broke into the open and was able to gulp air. But it was hard to keep her head above water. The current caught her again and she glanced off a rock. Splashing and kicking, she was swept down the river to a sharp bend. Below the bend, the water slowed into a deep pool. All but the top part of the pool was rimmed with ice.

Using all her strength, Nell managed to escape from the current at the head of the pool and reach the bank. Shaking with cold and exhaustion, she lay panting on the gravel. Then she got up, shook herself and looked around. She had made it across the river.

After a pause to get her bearings, she set off into the forest. Ahead, she heard the low-pitched call of a great horned owl *"Hoo! Hoo!*

Hoo! Hoo!" Farther on, Nell passed beneath the owl perched close to the trunk of a pine tree. Clicking its beak, the big predator swiveled its head and glared at her with yellow eyes until she was out of sight.

Overcome by exhaustion, Nell finally stopped to bed down in a patch of young evergreens at the edge of a hardwood bush. She was so tired that she went to sleep instantly.

She awoke with a start. Close by, one of the little fir trees was shaking violently. Ears erect, Nell stared at the tree. Quietly as a shadow she left her bed and circled behind the tree to see what was causing the commotion.

It was a snowshoe hare caught in a snare. Each time it struggled to get free of the noose, it shook the tree. Nell couldn't see the fine brass wire. Nor did she realize she had stumbled upon a trapline. All she knew was that the hare was acting strangely. Suspicious of its behavior, she lay down a safe distance away to see what would happen.

A few minutes later, the hare ceased to kick and lay still. Warily Nell approached the dead animal and sniffed it. Then she took the hare in her mouth and turned away with it. As she did so, the wire from the hare's neck to the tree went taut, and her meal was pulled from her mouth. Surprised, Nell clamped her teeth more firmly on the hare and gave it a hard tug. Once again it was pulled from her mouth.

At this point, hunger got the better of her. Ignoring the wire noose, she crouched in the snow and ate the animal on the spot.

The following night, padding through the spruce and fir trees, Nell came upon another hare caught in a snare. After making sure that no humans were in the vicinity, she ate it. The next day she combed the area again and found yet another trapped hare.

For Nell, the trapline was a bonanza. To get a meal all she had to do was take a stroll—and a hare caught in a snare tasted the same as any other.

◆

The trapper cursed and stared at the bloody remains in the snow. This was the third time he'd been robbed in as many days. Packsack slung across his shoulders, he trudged to the next snare. This one also held a dead hare, but the hare hadn't been touched.

Leaving the animal in the snare, the trapper

took from his packsack a steel-jaw trap. The trap had been soaked in chemicals to remove human scent. Kneeling, he scooped away the snow and placed the trap close to the carcass. After securing its chain to a metal stake driven into the frozen ground, he set the trap by standing on the levers attached to the coil springs. Then he sifted snow through his mitts to hide the trap and brushed away his footprints with a fir bough.

◆

Nell came upon the hare the following night. It looked the same as the others she had found, but her sixth sense told her something was wrong. She circled the dead animal from a distance, sniffing it from all angles. She detected no human odor, so she approached closer.

Now she could see the brass wire holding the hare, and each shiny whisker on its nose. A step at a time, she drew nearer to the bait.

When she reached the hare, she leaned forward to smell it. Then she grabbed it.

While she was eating, she worked her way around the carcass. As she did so, she kept moving her feet. At a certain moment, her right front foot touched the hidden trigger in the snow.

Snap!

The jaws of the trap closed on Nell's paw.

For a few seconds she didn't know what had happened. Then she felt the pain. She tried to jump back, but the chain held her fast. When she tried to run forward, the trap pulled her paw under her and she fell on her face. Terror-stricken, she struggled frantically to get free.

Soon her paw was numb. Panting from exertion, Nell tried to make sense of the situation. She could see that the jaws of the trap were clamped on her two front toes. Backing away from the stake, she tugged as hard as she could from different directions. It made no difference.

Her tug-of-war with the trap continued for more than an hour. By this time her strength was failing and she was ready to give up the struggle. Wearily she licked her imprisoned paw. Then, remembering Thor, she made one last desperate effort to escape. This time, her toes pulled free!

The next morning, when the trapper returned, he saw the story written in the snow.

The coyote had not only escaped, but had eaten the hare as well. Her tracks in the snow showed that she had been gone for hours.

All that Nell left behind was a small black toenail.

CHAPTER 9

Sunshine and Shadow

EXCEPT for a sore foot and the loss of her toenail, Nell was unhurt by the trap. But it gave her such a fright that she fled for two days with only brief stops to rest. On the third day she holed up under a fallen tree in a brushy ravine east of Lake Simcoe. She was so tired that she slept, curled nose to tail, from dawn till nightfall.

When she awoke, the sky was filled with stars, and the snow sparkled in the moonlight.

After she'd stretched and got her bearings, Nell's first thought was food. Senses sharpened by hunger, she found and caught a cottontail rabbit. Farther afield she came upon another cottontail crouched in a thicket. When she'd eaten the second rabbit, she felt comfortably full, and she started back to the ravine.

Her route took her along a fenceline bordering an overgrown farm pasture. As she padded along, her nose picked up a tasty odor.

Crawling under the rusty barbed wire, she followed the ribbon of scent to a clump of alders at the far end of the pasture. Carefully, she skirted the alders and then crept into them on her belly. There lay the source of the smell—a dead cow.

That night Nell watched the carcass from a distance. Memories of Thor's death, the ambush on the lake and the booby-trapped hare made her wary. The next night, she also hung back and saw a red fox slip in to feed, as well as a weasel and a number of smaller creatures. At dawn, a pair of crows drifted silently from the sky and landed beside the heifer.

Hunger overcame Nell's fear on the fourth night. Stalking from her hiding place, she bared her teeth at the fox, who instantly slunk into the alders. She might have chased the fox, but this time she was intent upon a meal.

◆

As the sun came up, the old man looked out the kitchen window.

He had made coffee on the wood stove. Now, cracked cup in hand, he watched the distant pasture, hoping to catch a glimpse of the black coyote.

While the first pink rays slid across the worn linoleum, he thought about the family homestead. The house needed a coat of paint, and another board was missing from the barn. The place had become too much for him. After his wife died last year, he'd simply lost interest. Nowadays he only kept a few beef cattle and a handful of chickens.

But seeing Nell the other morning had given his spirits a lift. That black critter sure was something. So graceful and wild. He didn't care if it ate the whole heifer so long as it didn't bother his hens or the barn cat. And it could stay as long as it liked.

He wouldn't tell his neighbors. Coyotes were considered pests and weren't protected by the law. Most of his neighbors would try to kill it. So nobody was going to know he had a coyote on his property. Besides, it was none of their business.

◆

Nell stayed around the farm until the end of March. Since leaving home in October she had become more cunning, tougher and self-reliant. At eleven months of age she was nearly full grown, with a thick, glossy winter coat.

Although food was plentiful and she felt safe on the farm, she was still restless and lonely. On a mild evening with a hint of spring in the air, she left the ravine and moved on. The old farmer would miss her.

The following day Nell stopped to rest in a small forest. At dusk, for the first time in ages, she heard a group of coyotes howling. For a moment she thought it was her family. Joyously she answered with several yips and a high-pitched howl—*Er-er-rooooo!*

There was silence and then an excited response from the distant pack, with several voices joining in the chorus of barks, yips and howls. Nell plotted the location of the coyotes and ran to meet them.

Nell came upon one of the strange coyotes in a clearing and stopped, wagging her tail. Seconds later, four other coyotes emerged from the shadows. An old female, the head of the pack, advanced toward her, stiff legged, with hackles up.

Nell was puzzled. Thinking that the leader might be teasing, she took a few steps forward, wagging her tail. The old female snarled a deep-throated warning that said, "This is our territory. Get out!" Nell knew better than to fight. Tail between her legs, she turned and fled.

Her flight took her to a golf course overlooking Lake Simcoe. Because it was early spring, there were no humans about, but there were plenty of mice and rabbits in the brush separating the fairways. However, the lack of protective cover and the open grassland made her feel uncomfortable. A few days later, she arrived in an area of small farms.

The second morning, when she was returning from a hunt, a farm dog saw her and raised the alarm. Soon she was being pursued by four dogs, one of which was very fast. The chase ended when she gave them the slip by going through a culvert and doubling back on her tracks. The culvert went under an abandoned railroad, which Nell followed south.

As she trotted along the overgrown right-of-way, she saw more signs of civilization—houses, buildings and standing machinery. This made her increasingly nervous. Several times the right-of-way crossed country roads, and she saw moving vehicles. Yet she couldn't turn back. The dogs might be lying in wait. To avoid being seen in the daylight, she holed up in another culvert.

At dark, she continued her journey. Soon she came to an intersection where a busy road crossed the rail line. Cars and trucks swished noisily past. The road terrified her, but on the other side of it was the safety and cover of the right-of-way.

Nell waited until the traffic thinned to make her move. Keeping an eye on a distant car, she started across the road.

Halfway across, she was blinded by the lights of a vehicle approaching from the opposite direction. She froze in mid-stride. Both cars kept coming. Nell wanted to run, but she was trapped by the lights. The lights grew brighter. There was a screech of brakes.

Thud!

The impact of the car tossed Nell into the ditch. The car stopped and the driver ran over. Several other cars stopped and another man, holding a flashlight, came over to where Nell lay unconscious.

"I really feel bad about hitting that dog. I tried to stop!"

The man with the flashlight shone the beam

on Nell. "It's still breathing." Then he bent down for a closer look. "Hey! I don't think that's a dog. Must be a coyote or a wolf."

"If it's a wild animal, what'll we do?"

One of the onlookers stepped forward. "The best place for it is the Toronto Wildlife Centre. If you'll give me a hand, I'll take it there."

Gently, the men carried Nell and laid her in the back of his car.

CHAPTER 10

A New Beginning

NELL was taken to the Toronto Wildlife Centre, a clinic that looks after injured and orphaned wild animals. When she was brought in, she was still unconscious. The vet who examined Nell looked into her eyes, listened to her heart and breathing, and checked her head for an obvious skull fracture.

Mary, a small woman with dark hair, stood beside the vet and watched intently. Mary was a senior member of the staff with a special fondness for coyotes.

"I've never seen a black coyote before," she said. "She's beautiful! But she's had a tough time. Look at the nick in her ear."

The vet pointed to Nell's hind leg. "That patch of white fur could be the scar from a bullet wound." Picking up Nell's paw, he added, "She's also missing one of her front toenails. They don't just fall off."

Nell was given an injection for concussion,

and her scrapes were cleaned and treated with an ointment to prevent infection. Then a slim tube was inserted in the vein of her foreleg to feed a solution to lessen shock.

Mary and an assistant carried Nell to another room. Here the coyote was eased into a cage and covered with a blanket. Before leaving, Mary draped a sheet over the cage to reduce the light and make her patient feel more secure. Nell lay motionless. The vet said he wasn't sure she would regain consciousness.

◆

Mary spent a restless night worrying about the black coyote. At the clinic the next morning, the first thing she did was check on Nell. Silently she entered the room, pulled back the sheet and opened the door of the cage. Holding her breath, she looked inside.

Nell must have sensed Mary's presence, for at that moment she woke. She had no idea where she was, but she was struck by the sharp smell of disinfectant. Painfully she opened her eyes. To her astonishment, a human was watching her. For an instant their eyes met. Nell tried to run, but she was too weak to stand. All she could manage was to crawl to the back of her cage.

Mary shut the cage door and tiptoed from the room. A few minutes later she returned with another woman. Kneeling, she reached into the cage and gently draped a towel around Nell's head. While she held Nell's jaws shut, her assistant slipped a leather dog muzzle over the coyote's nose. Then Mary removed the tube from Nell's leg and dressed her wounds. Fresh paper and a clean blanket were placed in the cage, as well as food and a bowl of water. To avoid alarming their patient, the women didn't speak and left as quietly as they had come.

Aside from a concussion—which gave her a headache for several days—Nell had no broken bones or serious injuries. But she was frightened by the sounds and smells of the clinic. In addition to the smell of disinfectant, there were other strange chemical odors. The sounds included human voices, the distress cries of an injured loon, baby foxes barking for their mother, and the honk of a Canada goose in the next room.

Mary visited Nell every day. Soon Nell

learned to recognize Mary's footsteps outside her door. Although humans were to be feared, Nell sensed that Mary was different, and that she was trying to help her.

For the first two days Nell was confined to her cage and fed special canned dog food. On the third day she was given a plastic dog crate to sleep in and allowed the run of the room. To prepare her for the wild, mice were added to her diet.

Mary placed a small tree in the middle of the floor to make Nell's room more homey. Nell usually stayed in her crate during the day, but she roamed around the room at night after the staff had gone home. When she was restless, she sometimes chewed the branches of the tree.

Nell recovered in four days. But, to be on the safe side—because she was going to return to the wild and she'd been on medication—she was kept longer. Although she had been picked up on the outskirts of the city, no one had seen a black coyote in the Toronto area, so it was assumed she came from the north.

On the eighth morning she was carried in her crate to a waiting van. Two volunteers drove north for several hours before leaving the highway and turning onto a series of dirt roads. Nell was miserable, swaying in her crate in the back of the noisy van, but she cheered up when they turned off the highway. Suddenly, through the exhaust fumes, she could smell the country!

Eventually the van bumped to a stop on a rutted logging road. The men opened the doors of the van. Heart thumping, Nell cowered at the back of her cage. The next thing she knew, the crate was lifted from the van, carried down the road and eased to the ground. The men opened the door of the crate and strolled back to their van.

For a minute Nell was too stunned to realize she could just walk out of her prison. Timidly she stepped into the sunlight. Then, with a glance over her shoulder at the men, she broke into a trot. Seconds later, with tail flying, she raced into the woods. She ran—first out of fear, and then for the sheer joy of it—until the shadows lengthened.

Nell found herself in hill country, with clear lakes and tall pines. Within a few days she got used to her new surroundings and learned the lay of the land. It was a pleasant place, but she was lonely. One evening she climbed to a rocky outcropping and howled in several directions. Ears cocked, she waited expectantly. She received no answer.

Nell hunted that night and rested the next day under a fallen tree. She was woken by a faint honking. Against the clouds she saw a skein of Canada geese beating their way north. As she watched them fade into the distance like a wisp of cobweb, she knew it was time to move on.

She set off at dusk. Her instinct told her to head east. There was no need to hurry, and she traveled at a comfortable pace. Each night her howls were met with silence. So she continued her quest.

◆

Two weeks after she was released, Nell walked into Algonquin Park. She didn't know that she had entered a forest area so vast that it contained more than two thousand lakes. Nor did she realize, when she crossed the invisible boundary, that shooting and trapping were prohibited in virtually all of the park.

That evening Nell howled once again. To

her delight, her call was answered! It was a young male. Nell and the unseen coyote exchanged more calls, then started toward each other. The stranger, hidden by a clump of cedars, loped past Nell. Catching his scent, Nell found his trail and barked to signal her position. They met at the edge of a small stream.

Her new friend's name was Smoke. Like Nell, he had left home the previous autumn, and he was alone in the world. Their meeting was a joyous one with lots of tail wagging and face sniffing.

Then, side by side, the two young coyotes—one smoky-gray and the other jet-black—trotted happily into the forest together.

Acknowledgments

First, I wish to thank Brent Patterson, one of Canada's foremost authorities on the Eastern coyote, for his generous counsel and advice. Brent fielded innumerable questions and lent me a lot of literature, including his own thesis.

Bob Bancroft, well-known biologist and field naturalist, also answered many questions, and lent me his personal collection of literature relating to *Canis latrans*.

Lloyd Duncanson, former curator of exhibits at the Nova Scotia Museum, patiently explained the rationale and demonstrated to me the workings of coyote traps. (Lloyd also made me a release cord, should one of my dogs be caught in a Conibear trap.)

Nathalie Karvonen, director of the Toronto Wildlife Centre, took time from her hectic schedule to show me over the premises and let me watch her treat a female coyote that had been hit by a car.

Dr. Rob Wentzell discussed a number of hypothetical accident scenarios and explained some of the veterinary procedures used in these cases.

My old friend, Michael Heney of Oshawa, researched Nell's route from Lake Simcoe to Toronto, and found an abandoned railway line for her to follow.

Finally, I must thank my editor, Shelley Tanaka, for her grace and skill in dealing with the manuscript.

Glenview Public Library
1930 Glenview Road
Glenview, Illinois

3 1170 00497 1929